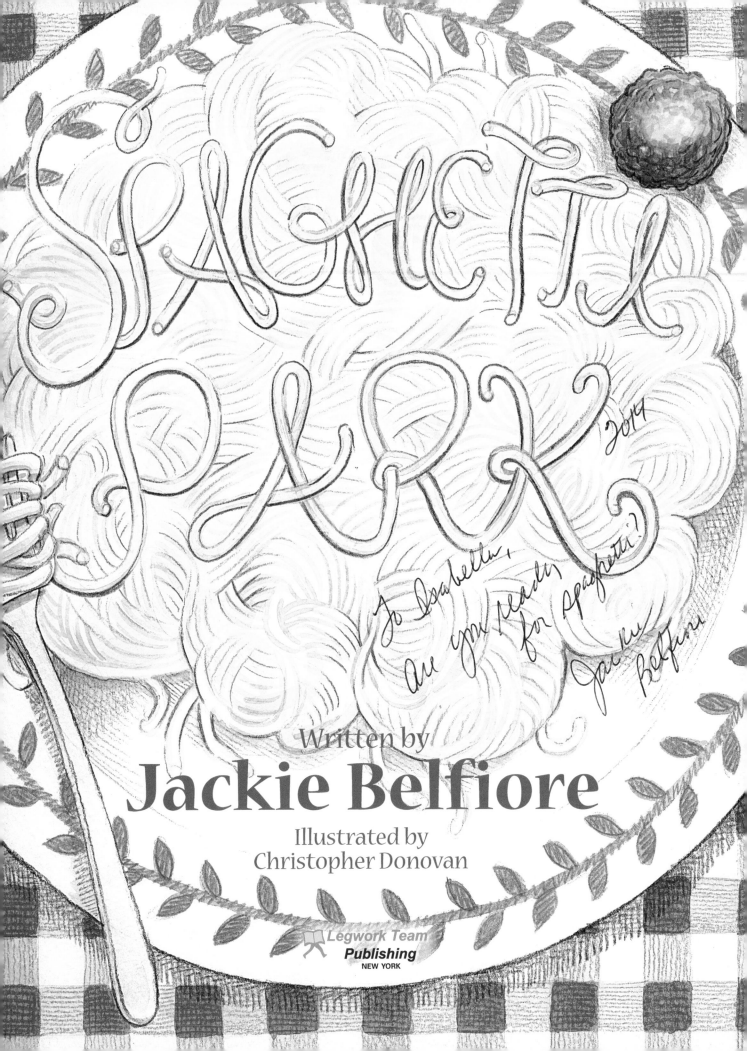

SPAGHETTI PARTY

2014

To Isabella,
Are you ready
for spaghetti?
Jackie Belfiore

Written by
Jackie Belfiore

Illustrated by
Christopher Donovan

Legwork Team
Publishing
NEW YORK

Legwork Team Publishing
Hauppauge, NY 11788
www.legworkteam.com
Phone: 631-944-6511

Disclaimer: This book, intended for young readers, is for educational and entertainment purposes only.

The ideas expressed herein are solely those of the author and do not necessarily reflect or represent those of Legwork Team Publishing or its staff. The publisher makes no endorsement as to the utility of this work and accepts no responsibility for reader conclusions, actions, or results.

It is strongly recommended that an adult supervise children at all times while they are preparing the recipes in this book. The publishers and copyright owners will not accept any responsibility for accidents that may occur when children are preparing these dishes.

First Edition 07/19/2013

Printed in the United States of America
This book is printed on acid-free paper

Illustrated by Christopher Donovan
Designed by Vaiva Ulenas-Boertje
Photos by Erica Angiolillo

Other books by Jackie Belfiore: "The Enchanted Florist"

Legwork Team
Publishing

To my children,
who are the beats of my heart,
for trying their best to respect Mom's need
to have a peaceful space to write.

To my family and friends,
whose encouragement, support, and
love of good food are truly treasured.

And to Spaghetti Park in Queens, NY,
which provided many sweet and
flavorful memories for our family.

I am also grateful
to the DiPietrantonio family for their
help with the recipe testing and tasting.

Let's go explore *Spaghetti Park*!
It's made from magical pasta that glows in the dark.

4

In the early morning, ziti songbirds are flying over and on
A rectangle-shaped court, lightly dusted with grated parmesan.

Bordering this, are strands of linguine the length of the court
Where two teams of four play bocce, an Italian lawn bowling sport.

Watch them as they aim for the pallino, the round smaller ball.
Points go to the player whose bocce meatball lands closest of all.

5

You can set yourself down on a ricotta-stuffed manicotti seat.
You'll love *Spaghetti Park*, which looks good enough to eat.

See small shell pasta flowers that are spread about everywhere
And schoolgirls who have Farfalle, bow tie-shaped pasta, fastened in
their windblown hair.

Cheerful children skillfully jump ropes of recycled spaghetti,
While others eagerly listen for their race to start, "On your mark, get ready

Huge, hovering trees are made from fusilli, colored ruby red, white, and blue.
Grab yourself a slice of Spaghetti Park Pie. It's delicious and nutritious too!

The Lemon Ice King of Corona on the corner of Penne Lane and Ziti Street
Serves refreshing Italian ices that can't be beat!

You'll see kids shout, "VICTORY," playing King of the Mountain
And then take lingering sips from lasagna-shaped water fountains.

Take a seat at the ravioli-topped tables to play cards or board games.
You don't have to be an expert to gain *Spaghetti Park* fame.

Tiny drops of Orzo occasionally shower down from above.
Gather enough for dinner by forming your hands into a glove.

You can eat the spinach tortellini growing on big blossoming bushes
As Moms clean remnants of pasta and sauce from contented kids' mushes.

9

Spaghetti Park, what an incredible place to be!
It's chock full of plentiful pasta, that can be shared between you and me.

Spaghetti Park is truly one of a kind.
How many pasta varieties on this page can you find?

Getting Ready

- Before you start, make sure it's okay with your grownup.
- Be prepared and review your recipe. Make sure you have all the ingredients and equipment you need before you begin.
- Wash your hands before you begin.
- Do not wear clothing that has long or baggy sleeves.
- If you have long hair, pin it back.
- Keep emergency numbers by the phone.
- Use a spoon rest—it helps keep your work area clean.
- Clean up as you go, this will help you stay organized and make the final clean up much easier.
- When using a knife, ask a grownup to help you. Always pick up a knife from the handle, and keep your fingers out of the way when cutting and chopping. Make sure your hands are dry, because the knife can be slippery if wet.
- Clean the top of canned goods before opening. There may be germs from where it is stored before it got to your home.
- Use potholders when handling hot pots, pans, and dishes. Make sure the oven mitts and potholders are dry. If they are wet or damp, it could cause steam. Steam burns! Be careful!
- If you touch something hot, immediately hold your hand under cool, not cold water.
- Turn off the burners before moving the pot or pan off the stovetop. Smother a pan fire by covering it with a pot cover, and turn off the heat. *NEVER* pour water on it!
- When stirring hot liquids, with one hand, hold the handle on the pot with a potholder or oven mitt, and then stir gently with your other hand. This will make the pot more steady and prevent hot liquid from splashing on you.
- Turn pan handles to the side of the stove to prevent from knocking into them.
- Always ask your grownup to help you carry heavy pans or drain hot food in a colander.
- When using a food processor, remember that the steel blades are very sharp. *NEVER* put your fingers inside the processor near the blade!

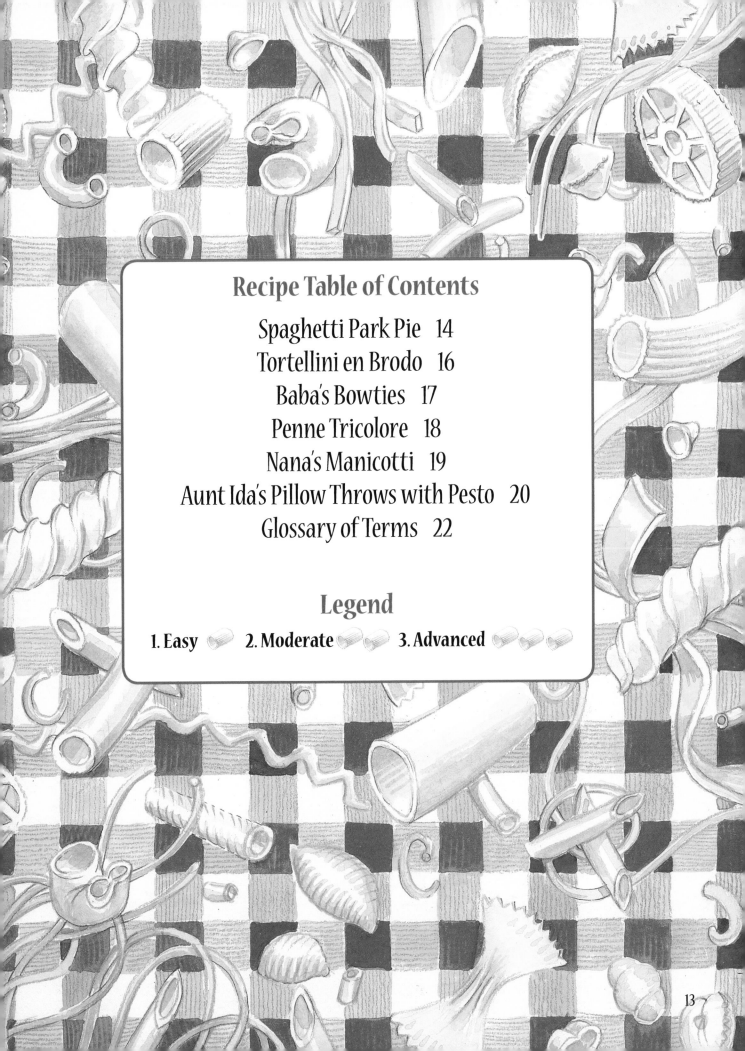

Recipe Table of Contents

Legend

1. Easy   **2. Moderate**   **3. Advanced**

Spaghetti Park Pie

Now that you know your pastas and some safety tips to apply,
Why don't you give these recipes a try?

I warmly recall making my very first Spaghetti Park Pie...

Total time: 45 minutes **Yield**: 8-10 slices **Difficulty Rating**:

FOR THE SAUCE:
You will need:
12 in. skillet
Large handled wooden spoon
Spoon rest
Sharp knife for chopping
Cutting board
Measuring cup
Can opener

Ingredients:
¼ cup extra virgin olive oil*
1 onion chopped
4 cloves of garlic, chopped
1 - 28 oz. can of crushed tomatoes
¼ cup water
6 leaves of fresh basil, stems removed
   and torn**
2 cups baby spinach, firmly packed
1 teaspoon of salt
½ teaspoon of ground black pepper

FOR THE PIE:
You will need:
Colander
4-6 quart pot for cooking pasta
Large mixing spoon
Large bowl for mixing cheese filling
   with pasta
10 in. deep dish pie plate or quiche pan
Oven mitts or potholders
Measuring spoons
Spatula

Ingredients:
½ lb. spaghetti
Dab of butter to coat pie plate
4 tablespoons of grated parmesan
   cheese (plus some for sprinkling)
1 lb. ricotta
2 cups shredded mozzarella
2 large eggs, lightly beaten

Directions:
- In a 12 in. skillet, heat the oil. (Make sure the oil is not too hot, if it is smoking, it's too hot!)
- Add onion and garlic, and then sauté over medium heat until onions are soft and garlic is lightly browned.
- Add crushed tomatoes.
- Then add ¼ cup of water to the empty can and swirl it around to make sure you get all of that tomato goodness out of the can, and add this to the skillet.
- Add basil, salt, and pepper.
- Cover and bring to a boil, about 5 minutes.
- Add spinach, lower heat, and simmer gently, stirring occasionally uncovered for 30 minutes.
- Taste and add salt and pepper, if needed. **No double-dipping please!**

While sauce is cooking:
- Coat the pie plate evenly with butter to prevent sticking.
- Preheat oven to 350 degrees.
- Cook spaghetti according to package directions, taste to make sure it's al dente (tender to the tooth), and drain well.
Remember it will be hot! Be careful!
- Let pasta cool.

In a separate large bowl:
- Mix the ricotta, grated cheese, eggs, and 1 ½ cups of shredded mozzarella.
- Add the drained pasta to the cheese mixture, and mix well.
- Add 3 cups of tomato sauce to pasta and cheese mixture, mix well.
- Pour into pie plate, pat it down, and sprinkle with grated Parmesan cheese.
- Make sure you scrape all of the contents of the dish out with a spatula.
- Bake for 30 minutes. Place a baking pan under the pie plate to keep any ingredients from dripping onto the bottom of the stove. This also makes it easier to take the pie in and out of the oven.
- Take pie out of oven and top with remaining ½ cup shredded mozzarella.
- Continue cooking until cheese melts, about 5 minutes.

Let the pie rest uncovered about 8-10 minutes before serving. This gives it time to set.

*¼ cup=4 tablespoons   **Tearing basil, rather than chopping releases more flavor and aroma*

Tortellini en Brodo

*You'll eagerly welcome Spinach Tortellini en Brodo.
It's a soup so delicious that you'll sing, "Do Re Mi Fa So La Ti Do!"*

Total time: 20 minutes **Yield**: 8 servings **Difficulty Rating**:

You will need:

3-4 quart pot
Large mixing spoon
Ladle
Oven mitts or potholders
Serving bowls
Measuring cup
Can opener, if using canned broth

Ingredients:

8 cups chicken broth
13 oz. package of spinach tortellini stuffed
   with cheese

Directions:

- Pour the broth into the pot.
- Cover and bring to a boil over high heat.
- Add the tortellini and lower the heat.
- Bring to a low boil, and simmer over medium heat, about 8 minutes.
- Taste the tortellini and make sure it's tender.
- Ladle the broth and tortellini into soup bowls and serve.

Serve this with crusty Italian bread and grated Parmesan cheese on the side.

As a variation, you can add ½ cup of shredded carrots and 2 cups of baby spinach to the pot when you add the tortellini.

Baba's Bowties

This is one of my favorites, farfalle with meat sauce.
Which was originally a flavorsome gesture given
by the wife of my boss.

Total time: 45 minutes   **Yield**: 4-6 servings   **Difficulty rating**:

You will need:

Colander
4-6 quart pot
12 in. skillet
Sharp knife for chopping
Cutting Board
Long-handled wooden spoon
Spoon rest
Serving bowls
Measuring cup
Oven mitts or potholders
Can opener

Ingredients

¼ cup extra virgin olive oil
3 large fresh garlic cloves peeled, then sliced
   or chopped
1 medium onion, peeled and chopped
1 lb. ground veal, beef, and pork combined
   (This is available in most grocery stores
   and local butcher shops. It is sometimes
   labeled meat loaf mix. You can substitute
   by using all ground beef if you'd like.)
6 large basil leaves, torn
1 - 28 oz. can crushed tomatoes + ¼ cup
   of water
1 teaspoon of salt
½ teaspoon of pepper
1 lb. farfalle (You can substitute farfalle
   for any pasta you like. I find that short
   pasta such as rigatoni or penne that are
   ridged also work well. The ridges help
   the sauce stick to the pasta.)

Directions:

- In a 12 in. skillet, heat oil (Make sure oil is
  not too hot, if it is smoking, it is too hot!)
- Add onion and garlic.
- Sauté over medium heat until onions are
  soft and garlic is lightly browned.
- Add ground meat combination and raise
  heat to high. Break up the meat so there are
  no large lumps.
- Sauté, stirring frequently until lightly
  browned and no longer pink, about
  8 minutes.
- Add crushed tomatoes.
- Add ¼ cup of water to the emptied
  tomato can and swirl it around to make
  sure you get all of the tomatoes out, add
  it to pot.
- Add basil, salt, and pepper.
- Lower heat, simmer uncovered, and stir
  occasionally for 30 minutes.
- Taste and add salt and pepper, as needed.

After the sauce has been simmering for
20 minutes:

- Cook farfalle according to package
  directions.
- Taste pasta to make sure it's tender.
- Place colander in sink and drain well.
- Pour pasta in bowl.
- Spoon the meat sauce over the cooked
  pasta and mix so that the pasta is covered.

Penne Tricolore

Penne with Asparagus is wholesome and good.
This recipe brings back tender memories from my early childhood.

I recall my mother at the stove, sautéing asparagus and sprinkling Parmesan cheese,
The thought of it still makes me weak in both knees.

Total time: 30 minutes   **Yield:** 4-6 servings   **Difficulty Rating:**

You will need:

- 4-6 quart pot
- 12 in. sauté pan
- Colander
- Large slotted spoon
- Spoon rest
- Large serving bowl
- Oven mitts or potholders
- Cutting board
- Paper towels
- Measuring spoons
- Measuring cup
- Knife for chopping and cutting

Ingredients:

- 1 bunch asparagus washed, trimmed, and cut
- 1 cup of cherry tomatoes
- 1 lb. penne pasta
- 1 tbsp. extra virgin olive oil
- 1 small onion, chopped
- 3 cloves garlic, peeled and chopped
- ¼ cup chicken broth
- ¼ lb. pancetta, diced
- 4 tablespoons of butter
- Grated Parmesan cheese for sprinkling
- Salt and pepper to taste

Directions:

- In a 12 in. sauté pan, heat oil on medium heat.
- Cook pancetta until crispy, about 8-10 minutes.
- Remove pancetta from pan with slotted spoon, place on paper towel to drain off fat.
- In the same pan, add butter, then onion and garlic, and sauté 4-5 minutes until onion is softened and garlic is lightly browned.
- Add asparagus and cherry tomatoes, and sauté for about 3 more minutes.
- Return pancetta to pan, add chicken broth, and simmer until bubbly, about 8 minutes.
- Add salt and pepper, if needed.
- While sauce is simmering, cook penne according to package directions.
- Taste to make sure the pasta is tender, and then drain well. (Remember it will be hot! Be careful!)
- Add pasta to large serving bowl, stir in asparagus mixture, and sprinkle with grated Parmesan.

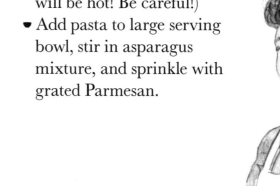

Nana's Manicotti

Here's a recipe for manicotti, a favorite of my sister-in-law.
I always make extra, friends and family always want more.

If you are in a hurry and there's less time than you thought,
There are stuffed manicotti shells ready-made, store-bought.

Total time: 1 hour   **Yield**: 6 servings   **Difficulty Rating**:

You will need:

Colander
6 quart pot to cook manicotti
12 in. skillet
9 in. x 13 in. baking dish
Large bowl to mix the cheese
Mixing spoon
Spoon rest
Oven mitts or potholders
Cutting board
Measuring cup
Can opener

Ingredients:

¼ cup extra virgin olive oil
1 onion, chopped
4 cloves of garlic, chopped
1 - 28 oz. can of crushed tomatoes
¼ cup water
6 leaves of fresh basil, stems removed
   and torn
1 teaspoon of salt
½ teaspoon of ground black pepper
12 manicotti shells
1 ½ lbs. ricotta
2 large eggs, lightly beaten
1 ½ cups shredded mozzarella
1 cup grated parmesan cheese plus
   some for sprinkling

Directions:

- In a 12 in. skillet, heat the oil.
- Add onion and garlic, and then sauté over medium heat until onions are soft and garlic is lightly browned.
- Add crushed tomatoes.
- Then add ¼ cup of water to the empty can and add this to the skillet.
- Add basil, salt, and pepper.
- Cover and bring to a boil, about 5 minutes.
- Lower heat and simmer gently, stirring occasionally, uncovered for 30 minutes.
- Taste and add salt and pepper, if needed. **No double-dipping please!**
- While sauce is cooking, preheat oven to 350 degrees.
- Cook manicotti shells according to package directions, and drain.
- Rinse pasta in cold water to make the manicotti easier to handle.
- In a separate large bowl, mix the ricotta, grated Parmesan cheese, eggs, and 1 cup of shredded mozzarella into a cheese mixture.
- Cover the bottom of the baking dish with approximately 1 cup of the tomato sauce.
- One at a time, fill the cooked and cooled manicotti shells with the cheese mixture and place them single layer in the dish. Do not overlap them!
- Cover the filled manicotti shells with remaining 1½ cups of tomato sauce, sprinkle with grated Parmesan cheese, and top with remaining ½ cup of shredded mozzarella.
- Bake for 30 minutes, or until the sauce is bubbly and the mozzarella is melted.
- Let the pie rest uncovered about 8-10 minutes before serving. This gives it time to set, and it will be easier to serve.

Aunt Ida's Pillow Throws with Pesto

Ravioli Pesto as an appetizer, what a great start!
Aunt Ida gave me this recipe straight from her heart.

Total time: 20 minutes   **Yield**: 5 appetizer portions   **Difficulty Rating**:

You will need:

Food processor with steel
  knife attachment
4-6 quart pot
Colander
Large mixing spoon
Spoon rest
Oven mitts or potholders
Measuring cup
Measuring spoons
Spatula

Ingredients:

4 cups fresh basil, washed, stems
  removed, firmly packed
¾ cups pine nuts
5 cloves garlic, peeled
¾ cup extra virgin olive oil
5 tbsp. grated parmesan cheese
1 stick of melted butter
13 oz. package of large
  square cheese ravioli
  (or you could use other
  shaped ravioli, with
  different fillings!)

Directions:

- Melt butter, and set aside to cool.
- Place basil, grated cheese, pine nuts, garlic, salt, and pepper in the food processor, using steel knife attachment.
- Pulse until mixture is pureed, stopping to scrape down the sides with the spatula. (Before scraping the mixture off the sides of the processor, turn it off, and wait for the blade to come to a complete stop. Then turn it back on and continue pulsing until a fine paste is formed.)
- With machine running, gradually add oil and melted butter through feed tube.

Then:
- Cook ravioli according to package directions.
  - Taste to make sure the ravioli is tender.
  - Drain well.
  - Gently toss the hot ravioli with the pesto sauce and coat well.

You will have leftover pesto sauce. To save it to use for another dish, you can place it in an airtight container, top it with extra virgin olive oil, and place it in the freezer for up to 3 months. Also, good quality ready-made pesto sauces are available at your local grocer.

Although the recipes on these pages number just a few,
Broaden your horizons, be adventurous, and try something new.

Ask someone to help you, always cook with a grownup at your side.
You can follow these recipes as they are, or just use them as a guide.

The choices are yours, add whatever you wish.
Enjoy your creation! It's your very own special dish.

Buon Appetito!

Glossary

Al-dente – "to the tooth," the pasta is cooked a little hard, but it's tender and not too soft and mushy.

Basil – a rich and fragrant herb whose leaves are used in cooking.

Capellini – derived from the Latin "capelli" for "hair." Capellini are very thin round pasta strands.

Chop – to cut into pieces.

Colander – a bowl-shaped kitchen utensil with holes in it, used for draining food such as pasta or rice.

Farfalle – a bow-tie shaped pasta that comes from the Italian word for butterfly.

Fusilli – long, thick, corkscrew-shaped pasta.

Garlic – an herb that is used in many dishes. Each bulb can be broken into smaller sections called cloves. Before you chop garlic, you must remove the papery covering that surrounds it.

Ladle – a long-handled utensil with a cup-shaped bowl for dipping or scooping.

Lasagna – wide, flat pasta shape and possibly one of the oldest varieties of pasta.

Linguine – means "little tongue," in Italian. It's a form of pasta, like spaghetti. It is wider than spaghetti and more flat.

Manicotti – large, tube-shaped pasta designed to be stuffed with meat, cheese, or vegetable fillings.

Mozzarella – a mild white Italian cheese that has a rubbery texture and is often eaten melted, as on pizza and in baked pasta dishes.

Orzo – a small rice-shaped pasta.

Packed – a measuring term that is often used with fresh basil, spinach, or parsley leaves. When a recipe calls for packed measurements, put ingredient in measuring cup, press down, and add until there is no more room in the cup.

Pancetta – known as Italian bacon. It is similar to bacon, but pancetta is cured, not smoked, which gives pancetta a milder flavor. Pancetta must be cooked before it is eaten.

Glossary

Parmesan cheese – (also known as Parmigiano Reggiano) – considered the king of cheeses, it is a hard cheese which is grated and sprinkled over pastas and salads.

Pesto – a sauce originating from Genoa in northern Italy, and traditionally consists of crushed garlic, basil, and pine nuts blended with olive oil and parmesan cheese.

Pre-heat – to heat an oven to a specific temperature before placing food inside.

Purée – food made into smooth sauce.

Ricotta – a soft, creamy, unsalted Italian cheese.

Rigatoni – large ribbed tubes about 1 ½ in. long. This chunky pasta is frequently used in oven baked dishes, but it can also be used in pasta recipes and salads. It is larger than penne and ziti, and sometimes slightly curved.

Rotelle – a wheel-shaped pasta that is also known as ruote. Rotelle is also used as the name of a corkscrew or spiral-shaped pasta, about 1 ½ in. long.

Sauté – to cook or brown in a pan containing a small quantity of butter, oil, or other fat.

Shredded – cut or torn into narrow pieces.

Simmer – to cook gently below, or just at, the boiling point.

Skillet – a long-handled saucepan or frying pan.

Small shells – called "conchiglie" in Italian, these shell pastas vary in size from small, sometimes used in soups, to an extra large variety that can be stuffed.

Spaghetti – long, thin, cylinder-shaped pasta made of flour and is of Italian origin.

Stir – to pass a spoon through a liquid in a circular motion to mix the contents.

Tortellini – ring-shaped pasta stuffed with meat or cheese; usually served in broth with cream, pasta sauce, or with salad dressing in a cold salad.

Tricolore – "Three colors" in Italian, and refers to the three colors of the Italian flag. Green represents hope, white represents faith, and red represents charity.

Yield – how many servings that the recipe will make, or people it will serve.

Ziti – medium-sized tubular pasta about 2 in. long and slightly curved. Ziti rigati has a ridged surface, while regular ziti is smooth.

About the Author

Jackie Belfiore is a mother, an author, and a lover of Italian food. Following her first book for children, *The Enchanted Florist*, Jackie hopes that this, her second book, will inspire young readers to learn to love cooking as much as she does.

Spaghetti Park

For more information regarding Jackie Belfiore and her work, visit her website: www.JackieBelfiore.com.

Additional copies of this book may be purchased online from www.LegworkTeam.com; www.Amazon.com; www.BarnesandNoble.com; or via the author's website: www.JackieBelfiore.com.

You can also obtain a copy of the book by ordering it from your favorite bookstore.

Manicotti bench

Close score

Ravioli topped table

This triangle-shaped park is named William F. Moore Park, in memory of the marine private who was killed in battle during WWI. It is affectionately known as "Spaghetti Park" to local residents and visitors, who come there to play bocce, cards, and enjoy Italian ices from the well known "Lemon Ice King of Corona," located nearby. The Lemon Ice King was started by the Befaremo family over 60 years ago, and offers a wide variety of Italian ices flavored by real fruit. It was also featured on the comedy series, *King of Queens*, starring Kevin James and Leah Remini.

Lemon Ice King flavors

Lemon Ice King

Photos: Erica Angiolillo

CPSIA information can be obtained
at www.ICGtesting.com
Printed in the USA
BVIC01n0107081113
335759BV00001B/1